Medallions

MEDALLIONS

❖

ZOFIA NAŁKOWSKA

Translated from the Polish and with an introduction by Diana Kuprel

NORTHWESTERN UNIVERSITY PRESS

Evanston, Illinois

Northwestern University Press
Evanston, Illinois 60208-4210

Printed in the United States of America

ISBN 0-8101-1742-8 (cloth)
ISBN 0-8101-1743-6 (paper)

Library of Congress Cataloging-in-Publication Data

Nalkowska, Zofia, 1885–1954.
    [Medaliony. English]
    Medallions / Zofia Nalkowska ; translated from the Polish and
with an introduction by Diana Kuprel.
    p. cm. — (Jewish lives)
    ISBN 0-8101-1742-8 (cloth : alk. paper) — ISBN 0-8101-1743-6
(pbk. : alk. paper)
    1. Holocaust, Jewish (1939–1945)—Poland—Fiction. 2.
Holocaust, Jewish (1939–1945), in literature. 3. World War,
1939–1945—Poland—Fiction. 4. Auschwitz (Concentration camp)
I. Title. II. Series.
PG7158.N34 M3413 2000
940.53'174386—dc21

                             99-048758

People dealt this fate to people.

❖

Contents

❖

Acknowledgments

I would like to thank the following people who offered invaluable advice and suggestions during the translation process: Louis Iribarne, Henry Dasko, Antony Polonsky, and Madeline Levine. A version of the introduction was published in *POLIN: Studies in Polish Jewry* (1999).

Introduction

The final entry in Zofia Nałkowska's *Dzienniki czasu wojny* (1970, *Wartime Diaries*) is dated 10 February 1945: "Borejsza proposes that I become the president of the Commission for the Investigation of War Crimes in Auschwitz."[1] This conclusion to the diaries, and the writer's acceptance of a position on the Commission, mark the genesis of Nałkowska's literary Holocaust memorial, *Medaliony* (*Medallions*). The Commission was established immediately after the war to investigate Nazi war crimes committed on Polish soil, and Nałkowska's work in this area, together with her own experience of living in occupied Warsaw, would influence her profoundly.

A novelist, playwright, short-story writer, and essayist, Zofia Nałkowska (1884–1954) was the daughter of Anna and Wacław Nałkowski, a prominent Warsaw scholar and publicist. She was brought up in the rarefied atmosphere of the contemporary avant-garde. In her youth, she was part of the Young Poland (Młoda Polska) movement that defined the country's fin de siècle cultural world.[2] During the interwar period she served as an active member of the Polish PEN Club, became the first female member of the Polish Academy of Literature in 1937, and was patron of a popular Warsaw literary salon (Zespół Literacki Przedmieście).

A series of historic catastrophies, starting with the 1905 Russian Revolution, continuing through the First World War, and ending with the genocide of the Second World War, shattered Nałkowska's world. In a 1929 article she describes how her view of reality was changing: "Ever since I was a child, I've been surrounded by books. The adults around me talked about scholarship. Our friends were scholars or writers. I thought it was like this everywhere, that the world of thoughts and ideas constituted the only reality. Later, I was shocked to learn that it was otherwise."[3]

The burning of the Warsaw ghetto during the Second World War served as a definitive break: "Nothing of the former world holds true anymore. Nothing has remained" (7 May 1943).[4] In her *Wartime Diaries*, Nałkowska expresses the impact that ubiquitous death has had on her during this critical period: "The dead. The dead. The solemn march-pasts of the resigned. The leaps into the flames. The leaps into the abyss. The woman in the garden listening to the trickling droplets. The boy at the window. The children clung onto. I cannot bear these thoughts. I am changing because of them" (28 April 1943).[5]

This change, which can be charted in her *Wartime Diaries*, involved a heightening consciousness of her obligation as a writer to bear witness to what was going on around her and to fix in words all that was being wiped off the earth to prevent it from vanishing without a trace. Prior to the Warsaw Ghetto Uprising, in a diary entry dated 15 January 1943, Nałkowska describes her task as writer within a strictly personal context: "The only reason I've ever had to write has been the desire to preserve life, to keep it from being lost or destroyed. I always find it hardest to write about events, to talk about someone else's affairs. It turns out in the end that I preserve only myself. [The thought of] passing without a trace fills me with fear."[6] In 1936 the Polish avant-garde writer Witold Gombrowicz noted this tendency toward self-reference as he comments glowingly on her elegant style, which he equated with her self:

> There is a good reason why her style is the iron capital of her art and one of the very few exportables in our national literature. Nałkowska herself is style and there is no difference between the style of her books and her life. Even though she is widely regarded as an intellectual, no puzzles really exist for her. In the final analysis, what is essential to her is only the attitude taken toward the puzzle, the particular feeling that a problem evokes when it comes up against her person. In spite of appearances to the contrary, she is a great egoist for whom the whole matter comes down to this—namely, how to rescue her own humanity from the snares of contemporary civilization.[7]

Another diary entry, written a year after the Warsaw Ghetto Uprising and the razing of the ghetto district, shows a radical alteration in
Nałkowska's realization of the depth of her responsibility to the human drama under way around her, and her affirmation of the ethical
task of representing the occupation and the Holocaust. At the same
time, Nałkowska acknowledges the impossibility of portraying the
whole, and that, as a consequence, certain aspects are consigned inevi-
tably to the realm of silence: "Air raids wipe out towns. People die in
various ways, under every possible circumstance. Nothing remains.
And the whole thing for me can be encapsulated in this. Namely, that
I write. And on this it ends. This is everything. And yet it is. By
writing, I salvage that which is. The rest is beyond my reach. The
rest is relegated to silence" (May 1944).[8] This tension between writing and silence reappears in *Medallions* and becomes transfigured into
the ethical issue of speaking versus remaining silent.

In 1945, after having survived five years of Nazi occupation in
Warsaw, Nałkowska joined the editorial staff of the literary weekly
Kuźnica (*Forge*) and became a member of the Commission for the In-
vestigation of Nazi War Crimes; she went on to serve as a member of
the National Council (Krajowa Rada Narodowa), the Legislature
(Sejm Ustawodawczy, from 1947), and the Diet of the Polish People's
Republic (Sejm PRL, from 1952).[9] The Commission was based in
Łódź and established, for partly self-interested reasons, by the Com-
munists who had seized power in Poland while they carried on a sav-
age political struggle with the Polish Home Army (Armia Krajowa).
Its work took her to Oświęcim-Brzezinka (Auschwitz-Birkenau),
Sztutowo (Stutthof, near Gdańsk), Majdanek (near Lublin), Tre-
blinka, and to numerous other sites of extermination.

Considered a masterpiece in Holocaust world literature, *Medallions*
(written in 1945 and first published in 1946) was born from Nałkowska's wartime and Commission experiences. It also represents the cul-
mination of her literary evolution[10] from flowery description and a
focus on aesthetic concepts of personality in *Kobiety* (1906, *Women*),
Książę (1907, *The Prince*), and *Lustra* (1913, *Mirrors*) to a concern with
the fate of nations and peoples in *Tajemnica krwi* (1917, *The Secret of
Blood*); to the simple narration of facts and the everyday lives of ordinary people in *Dom nad łąkami* (1925, *A House in the Meadows*); and

to the reevaluation of fact-based and documentary genres in *Choucas*
(1927). Her work in the 1930s would prove especially significant as
a background to her postwar concerns. *Granica* (1935, *The Boundary
Line*) focuses on how character is determined externally by social roles
and cultural patterns. *Ściany świata* (1931, *The Walls of the World*) is a
series of prison stories contemplating the social and existential causes
of criminality. *Dzień jego powrotu* (1931, *The Day of His Return*) is a
play about the potential for criminal behavior latent in everyone, and
Niecierpliwi (1939, *The Impatient Ones*) is a philosophical novel present-
ing her attitudes toward evil, suffering, and death.

Even though there was an obvious evolution in subject matter toward her antifascist work, the raw material that confronted Nałkowska during the hearings required that she take an innovative approach
to writing and that she adopt a different perspective.[11] Commenting
on the intimate relation between theme and form, she discusses the
demand placed on her to find a new means by which to represent
the Holocaust:

> I maintain that it is the theme . . . that determines the appropriate man-
> ner of representation. I didn't work for the Commission for the Investiga-
> tion of Nazi War Crimes right after the war in order to find material for
> a new book. When I wrote *Medallions*, I wasn't conscious of creating a
> new technique, a different literary mode from my other books. The theme
> alone, which is so difficult to grasp, so impossible to deal with emotion-
> ally, demanded that I use this realistic form of expression.[12]

Medallions is one of the first, and most important, literary accounts
to take up the challenge to represent the Nazi machinery of genocide.
Comparable to it in significance stands the work of Nałkowska's com-
patriot Tadeusz Borowski, whose compelling collection of short
stories, *This Way for the Gas, Ladies and Gentlemen*, derives from his
personal experiences as a prisoner in Auschwitz and Dachau. Włodzimierz Wójcik evaluates the importance of *Medallions* in the context
of Polish Holocaust literature: "Despite the obvious fact that none
of the writers [e.g., Andrzejewski, Putrament, Rudnicki] was in the
position to tell the whole truth about the Nazi crimes, it must be
emphasized that perhaps two people, Borowski and Nałkowska, did
succeed in showing the most important aspects [of these crimes]."[13]

Avoiding the tendency to mythologize the victims as either heroes or martyrs,[14] *Medallions* offers instead a concise, severely elegant witness to what people experienced in Poland during the war. In reference and deference to the writer's accomplishment here, Jarosław Iwaszkiewicz comments, "Only from deep wisdom and great feeling are such works, which on the surface seem restrained and cool, but in reality are burning and passionate, born."[15]

The book consists of seven short reportages, each merely a few pages long, and one summation. In the summation, entitled "The Adults and Children of Auschwitz," Nałkowska gathers the various threads together and uses the facts to indicate the enormity of the crime and the ultimate compromise of humanity. In the process, Poland is portrayed as a land where every site has become as good a place as any for the task of disposing of the "undesirable" element. Her terse, sometimes fragmented, witness reports take the form of official testimony, private interviews, and chance conversations, and are interjected sparingly with objective authorial commentary. The protagonists are allowed to speak for themselves, from their own limited understanding of the human drama; at the same time, they speak on behalf of millions, with each "medallion" becoming a permutation on the principal theme that "people dealt this fate to people."[16] Ewa Pieńkowska sums up:

Zofia Nałkowska's "economical booklet," written directly after the war in the spring and summer of 1945, holds a special place in the abundant and varied canon of so-called camp literature. By preserving the authenticity of facts and the deeply personal character of individual experiences, and by remaining true to documentary prose and the memoir, . . . she goes beyond ordinary reportage. However, she does import intellectual and literary frameworks that allow her to generalize from individual experiences and bestow an objectivity on them. The moral theme of vigilance and protest against the psychological devastation by fascism which is inscribed in the factual accounts, together with . . . the marked conviction—and how early on!—that there are experiences that time does not erase, that memory preserves ("The Cemetery Lady")—[all these features of her writing] set the line of inquiry followed by writers of the younger generation, [such as] Tadeusz Borowski and Tadeusz Różewicz.[17]

Using the documentary form, Nałkowska seeks to restore to the victims and witnesses of genocide a voice that had been almost silenced by the Nazis. She asserts the adequacy and reliability of the survivors' own words to speak for the experience ("Dwojra Zielona"). And she engages in the painstaking work of preserving what remains from the oblivion that the passage of time, overgrown graves, natural decomposition ("The Man Is Strong"), and orders from the top (undermined by the soap "recipe" left hanging on the wall in "Professor Spanner") threaten. Lore Shelley explains the ethical appropriateness of using the literary strategy of the eyewitness account to represent the Holocaust:

> Abandoning the general view of the anyway too gigantic whole in favor of an essential detail establishes the right of the individual not to be overlooked and conforms to John Ruskin's view of obtaining the facts right from the source: "The only history worth reading is that written at the time of which it treats, the history of what was done and seen, heard out of the mouths of the men who did and saw."[18]

Medallions presents the reader with more than a mere historical record. It conveys not only the words but also the intonations, silences, gestures, postures, and actions of the witnesses as they struggle to relate their experiences. Nałkowska offers a startlingly immediate performance that repeats the past event in the testimonial present, demonstrating how it persists in the consciousness and conscience of these individuals. The book thus preserves for its readers the traces of the original experiences by inscribing human suffering in paper epitaphs.

Medallions portrays a terror-filled time ruled by chance, when one could never tell when, where, or under what circumstances one would die ("The Cemetery Lady" and "Dwojra Zielona"). "By the Railway Track," the story of a Jewish woman who chose uncertain death over certain death by escaping through a hole in a moving train, reverses this by establishing the certitude of death with the opening line: "Yet another person now belongs to the dead: the young woman by the railway track whose escape attempt failed." The account then transposes the dying woman's feelings of terror, pain, and solitude onto the landscape, which is described as desolate, empty, and menacing to both the woman and the villagers.

In this context, it is important to note that the refusal of the villagers in "By the Railway Tracks" to help the wounded Jewish woman was not a simple sign of anti-Semitism. During the German occupation, in Poland alone among the occupied European countries, giving aid to a Jew was punishable by death. Not only the individual who helped, but his or her entire family, even the whole village, could receive this sentence or be sent to the concentration camp. Nevertheless, according to the Yad Vashem Institute in Jerusalem, the greatest number among those honored for saving Jews during the war were Poles.

"The Hole," "The Visa," and "The Adults and Children of Auschwitz" show how humanity can be reduced to bestiality, to cannibalism, and to playing a deadly game of hunter and hunted. As the survivor in "The Hole" divulges about women sent without food to the bunker as punishment for any minor offense: "'They did eat, though . . . Once, one of them moved her jaw. Another had bloodied fingernails. Please, madame, that was severely punished! But at night they would eat the flesh of those corpses!'"

Nałkowska reveals how cruelty works to strangle moral sensibility. In "Professor Spanner," the young man from Gdańsk who is being questioned by the tribunal about activities in the Anatomy Institute is considered not so much a criminal as someone who has been desensitized to the moral reprehensibility of his actions. He speaks earnestly and unsensationally about the executions and the requisitioning and preparation of corpses, and refers to the production of soap from human fat in terms of the Germans' ability to "make something—from nothing."

"Professor Spanner" also exposes the victory of fascism over the German intelligentsia. The visiting German professors remain unperturbed when confronted with their colleague's activities at the Anatomy Institute. Their explanations for his motives as stemming from either obedience to the Party or the wish to aid the German economy suggest that they, too, could have been co-opted by the fascist genocidal machinery.

Nałkowska captures the critical moment when death is no longer an individually experienced event but has become collective and widespread. "The Cemetery Lady" opens by contrasting two instances of death by leaping from a window (suicide and escape) and two types of cemeteries: the traditional site where the burial ritual is enacted and the burning ghetto where people die en masse. She thereby establishes a breach between two spatial realities delimited by the wall, and two temporal realities of before and during the war. The reach of the genocidal action comes across vividly in "The Visa," where the narrator compares the fortitude of the Yugoslav, French, Dutch, Belgian, Greek, Polish, Gypsy, and Russian women in the camp. And in "The Man Is Strong," the uncovering of a child's knuckle, a Greek matchbox, and papers from some unspecified foreign pharmacy signifies the indiscriminateness of the murder of people of all ages and nationalities.

The stories also offer some hope. They express the belief that life has value in and of itself, and that people must bear witness to events, even in the face of certain death and mounting loss. "Dwojra Zielona," for example, paints a portrait of a woman who fought tenaciously to stay alive in order to tell, but who could not bear to go on alone, and who voluntarily followed the others to the concentration camp.

Yet, even more revealing than what is stated outright is what remains relegated to silence; trapped in the interstices of partially enunciated truths and fragmented testimonials; broken by emotion, shame, ignorance, fear, shock; noted by the narrator only in creases drawn across the forehead, outpourings of tears, or sagging shoulders—that is, in the physical traces of an event as it is relived mentally ("The Hole" and "The Man Is Strong"). Henryk Vogler aptly remarks that *Medallions* "speaks with silence. Silence has value there where even the most powerful words prove too weak."[19]

Through its objective, multifaceted witnessing, *Medallions* consciously and thematically engages the reader's intellect, emotions, imagination, and judgment in the critical detection of "distortions, assumptions, discrepancies, and misperceptions,"[20] so that he or she may begin to fill in the unsaid and the unsayable, and thereby render it real and present once again. This makes the book unusual for its time and interesting for ours, over fifty years after the fact and the book's first publication, and even with our by now abundant knowledge of the Holocaust. To quote from "The Cemetery Lady":

[R]eality is endurable because it is selective. It draws near in fragmented events and tattered reports, in echoing shots, in the distant smoke drifts, in the fires which, history cryptically says, "turn into ashes." This reality, at once distant and played out against the wall, is not real—that is, until the mind struggles to gather it up, arrest, and understand it.

The reader is put in the same position as the narrator in "The Visa" who is faced with the witness's deliberately provocative equation of Jews and vermin. Nałkowska does not make moral judgments; she leaves that to her readers. She lets the witnesses, survivors, and participants implicate themselves—as do Professor Spanner's soap-making assistant and the visiting German professors, or the cemetery lady, who turns murder into an act of self-preservation: "'If the Germans lose the war, the Jews will kill us all. You don't believe me? Listen, even the Germans say so . . . and the radio, it says so too.'" Each of Nałkowska's medallions confronts us with what Harold Kaplan, in *Conscience and Memory*, refers to as our own "consciousness struggling for comprehension," with the awareness that "[i]t may be that only questions are possible, interrupted answers, abortive explanations, and yet, one hopes, there may be judgment, something that touches conscience as well as memory, but with sharpness, unclouded by abstraction and generalizing formulae."[21]

Notes

1. Zofia Nałkowska, *Dzienniki czasu wojny* (Warsaw: Czytelnik, 1970), 399. All English translations from Polish texts are mine.
2. The Young Poland movement (1890–1918) was flanked by positivism in the nineteenth century and the twenty-year interwar period (1918–39) in the twentieth. Its major centers were in Kraków, Warsaw, and Lwów.
3. Nałkowska, "O sobie," *Wiadomości Literackie* 47 (1929).
4. Nałkowska, *Dzienniki czasu wojny,* 280.
5. Nałkowska, *Dzienniki czasu wojny,* 279.
6. Nałkowska, *Dzienniki czasu wojny,* 267.
7. Witold Gombrowicz, "O stylu Zofii Nałkowskiej," in *Proza (Fragmenty), Reportaże, Krytyka: 1933–1939* (Kraków: Wydawnictwo Literackie, 1995), 207.
8. Nałkowska, *Dzienniki czasu wojny,* 337.
9. Biographical details are taken from "Nota biograficzna," in Nałkowska, *Medaliony* (Warsaw: Kama, 1994), 73–74.

10. For an overview of Nałkowska's literary development, see Helena Zaworska, *"Medaliony" Zofii Nałkowskiej* (Warsaw: Państwowe Zakłady Wydawnictw Szkolnych, 1969); Włodzimierz Wójcik, *Zofia Nałkowska* (Warsaw: Wiedza Powszechna, 1973).

11. Kazimierz Brandys, in "'Medaliony' Zofii Nałkowskiej," *Kuźnica* 4 (1947), comments on this change: Nałkowska, "the discoverer of vast regions in human psychology, stands helpless before humanity in *Medallions*, as though she understood that explicating this world's secrets vis-à-vis the psychology of the individual was just not appropriate. This is her first book in which the human being is not penetrated by the writer, but only described" (cited in Nałkowska, *Medaliony*, 12).

12. Nałkowska, "Pisarze wobec dziesięciolecia," *Nowa Kultura* 2 (1954).

13. Wójcik, *Zofia Nałkowska*, 373. These writers' works, which touch on different aspects of the war experience and are of varying degrees of artistic merit, all (with the exception of Borowski's) speak about the tragic fates of individuals faced with an unusual test of character, endurance, and courage. *Medallions*, by contrast, Wójcik argues, is one of the few to represent "the commonness of the occupation experience" (ibid., 372). See also Kazimierz Wyka's similar conclusion in "Sprawy prozy," *Szkice literackie i artystyczne*, vol. 2 (Kraków, 1956); cited in Nałkowska, *Medaliony*, 7–8.

14. Piotr Kuhiwczak comments on popular representations of the concentration camps, to which he contrasts Tadeusz Borowski's *Pożegnanie z Marią* and *Kamienny świat* (works known in English as *This Way for the Gas, Ladies and Gentlemen*) and Primo Levi's *Survival in Auschwitz* and *The Reawakening*: "To circumvent such uncomfortable questions, some prefer to suppose that all inmates of Nazi concentration camps were people of outstanding character, either national heroes or born martyrs. Popular fictitious representations of prison camps peddle the same mythology. Almost invariably they centre on successful escapes, like that presented in the recent American film about Sobibor, for example, well-organized resistance networks, and numerous acts of individual heroism. It seems that a hero dying for a noble cause is still preferable to a survivor who manages to preserve a minimum of human integrity; that a prisoner who declares his/her trust in the goodness of the human heart against all odds, scores more points than a prisoner who is skeptical about human nature and manages to stick to just one of the commandments Pawelczynska found prevailing at Auschwitz—'Do not harm your neighbour and, if at all possible, save him'" ("Beyond Self: A Lesson from the Concentration Camps," *Canadian Review of Comparative Literature* [September 1992]: 398). Although Nałkowska is not speaking from personal experience of the concentration camps, her *Medallions* falls into the same category as Borowski's and Levi's works.

15. Jarosław Iwaszkiewicz, "Do Zofii Nałkowskiej," in *Cztery szkice literackie* (Warsaw, 1953); cited in Nałkowska, *Medaliony*, 13.

16. The initial formulation of the theme is found in the *Wartime Diaries* in the entry dated 28 July 1944.

17. Ewa Pieńkowska, "Zofii Nałkowskiej życie i twórczość" (Warsaw, WSiP); cited in Nałkowska, *Medaliony*, 5.

18. Lore Shelley, compiler, translator, and editor, *Experiments on Human Beings in Auschwitz and War Research Laboratories: Twenty Women Prisoners' Accounts* (San Francisco: Mellen Research University Press, 1991), 3.

19. Henryk Vogler, "Medaliony ryte w słowie," *Z notatek przemytnika* (Warsaw, 1957); cited in Nałkowska, *Medaliony*, 10.

20. James Wilkinson, in "A Choice of Fictions: Historians, Memory, and Evidence," *PMLA* 3, no. 1 (January 1996), discusses this critical tendency to read beyond what is expressly stated with respect to the work of the historian: "'Even in the most resolutely

intentional evidence,' [Marc] Bloch notes, . . . 'what the text tells us expressly has today ceased to be the primary object of our attention. We ordinarily show much more interest in what it reveals without meaning to.' . . . The gap between the witness's initial intent and the historian's final discovery lies in the historian's ability to detect distortions, assumptions, discrepancies, and misperceptions through a critical reading of the evidence" (85).

21. Harold Kaplan, *Conscience and Memory: Meditations in a Museum of the Holocaust* (Chicago: University of Chicago Press, 1994), xi.

Medallions

Professor Spanner

It was our second visit there that May morning. The day was pleasant and fresh. The brisk sea breeze recalled years long since passed. Beyond the trees lining the wide asphalt avenue grew a hedge, and beyond the hedge a spacious courtyard spread out. We already knew what we would see.

Two elderly gentlemen, "colleagues of Doctor Spanner," accompanied us this time. Both were professors, doctors, scientists. One was tall and gray-haired, with a thin, noble face; the other was just as tall, but stout and heavy, with a fleshy face that exuded benevolence and compassion.

They were dressed alike, not as we dress, but rather provincially, in long, black spring coats of good wool and soft, black hats.

A modest, unplastered, brick cottage stood in the corner of the courtyard, off to the side—an inconspicuous pavilion next to the huge edifice housing the Anatomy Institute.

We entered the gloomy spaciousness of the basement first. The light, refracted through the high-set windows, bathed the dead, lying as they lay yesterday. The young, cream-colored, naked bodies, hard as sculptures, were perfectly preserved, despite their months-long wait for the moment when they would no longer be required.

They reposed in long, concrete, sarcophagus-like basins with raised lids, stacked one on top of the other—arms abandoned to the side, not positioned on their breasts in accordance with the funeral rite, and heads detached from the torsos so evenly that the bodies appeared to be carved from stone.

In one sarcophagus, the so-called headless "sailor" lay prostrate on a heap of cadavers. He was an impressive youth, as big as a gladiator. The silhouette of a ship was tattooed on his broad chest. Across the contour of the two masts hung the sign of vain faith: God is with us.

One after the other, we filed past basins filled with corpses. The two foreigners strolled past and looked, too. Being doctors, they understood better than we did what this meant. The university's Anatomy Institute required a supply of fourteen cadavers; there were three hundred and fifty here.

Two vats contained only decapitated, shaved heads piled one on top of the other—human faces like potatoes poured onto the ground, some on their side as though they were resting on a pillow, others facing down or up. They were yellowish, smooth, perfectly preserved, evenly severed at the neck, as if they, too, had been cut from stone.

In the corner of one vat lay the small, cream-colored head of a boy who couldn't have been more than eighteen years old when he died. His dark, somewhat slanted eyes weren't closed, the eyelids were only slightly lowered. The full mouth, of the same color as the face, bore a patient, sad smile. The strong, straight brow was raised as though in disbelief. In this most odd and inconceivable position, he awaited the world's final verdict.

Further on even more corpse-filled basins were lined up, and near them vats of halved, quartered, and skinned men. Only one basin, located apart from the others, was filled with the remains of a few women.

In this basement, we could also see some empty basins, barely finished and still lidless, indicating that the supply of cadavers required for the living was insufficient, that they intended to scale up the whole production.

Later, accompanied by the professors, we crossed over to the brick cottage. There, on the cooled hearth, stood a huge cauldron brimming with a dark liquid. Someone familiar with the premises poked under the lid and retrieved a boiled human torso, skinned and dripping with the liquid.

Two other cauldrons stood empty. But close by, in a glass cupboard, boiled skulls and femurs were arranged neatly in a row.

We also saw a chest with layers of thin pieces of prepared human skin, stripped of its fat, some vials of caustic soda on a shelf, a cauldron with a brew mounted on the wall, and a huge stove for burning scraps and bones.

Finally, pieces of rough, white soap and a pair of metal molds stained with dried soap lay on a high table.

We didn't climb up to the attic to survey the sprawling heap of skulls and bones this time. We stopped briefly in one part of the courtyard to view the remnants of three burned-down buildings, metal ovens of the crematorium variety, and countless pipes and tubes. It was common knowledge that the brick cottage had been set on fire twice. Each time, however, the fire had been spotted and extinguished just in time.

We strolled out together, accompanied by the professors, who immediately broke away, escorted by a stranger.

2

A young, thin, pale man with lively, blue eyes, escorted from prison to the inquest, is testifying before the Commission. He has no idea what we want of him.

He speaks with grave consideration. He speaks in Polish, but with a foreign accent.

He says he comes from Gdańsk. He completed elementary school, then did six more grades and received his high school diploma. He'd been a volunteer, a Boy Scout. During the war, he was captured, but he escaped. He worked shoveling snow; later he worked in a munitions factory. Again he escaped. The incident, for the most part, took place in Gdańsk.

A German came to live at his mother's house after his father had been sent to the concentration camp. The German secured a job for him at the Anatomy Institute. That was how he met Professor Spanner.

Professor Spanner was writing a book on anatomy and employed him to prep cadavers. Spanner taught an introductory course at the university. All the research would be used for his book. His associate, Professor Wohlmann, was also working, though on what he couldn't say . . .

The outbuilding of the smokehouse was completed in 1943. Spanner then requisitioned machines for separating meat and fat from bones. Skeletons were to be made from the bones. In 1944, he ordered the students to set aside the fat from the corpses. Every evening after class, after the students had left, the workers would gather up platters of fat. The veins and flesh were placed on other platters. They either disposed of or burned the flesh. But the townsfolk complained about the stench to the police, so the professor ordered that the burning be carried out at night.

The students were also told to clean the skin, later the fat, later still, following the directions specified in the "manual," the muscles from the bones. This fat was left to lie all winter, and later, after the students left, it was converted into soap over the course of five or six days.

Professor Spanner also collected human skin. Working with the older prepper, von Bergen, he would prepare it and make something out of it.

"The older prepper, von Bergen, was my immediate supervisor. Professor Spanner's deputy was Doctor Wohlmann. Professor Spanner was a civilian, but he volunteered for the SS as a doctor."

The prisoner was unaware of Doctor Spanner's current whereabouts.

"Spanner left in January 1945. When he went away, he ordered us to continue working on the fat collected during the previous semester, to properly clean the skeletons and cook the soap, and to tidy up so the place looked decent. He didn't tell us to get rid of the recipe. Maybe he forgot. He said he'd come back, but never did. His mail was forwarded to him at Halle an der Saale, Anatomisches Institut."

While testifying, he sits on a chair against the wall, opposite the window, in the light. He is completely transparent in his careful deliberation, in his conscientious desire to convey everything in precise detail and to not overlook anything. He is alone. We, the members of the Commission, local officials, judges, are many.

In his earnestness, he leaves certain details fuzzy.

"What is the recipe?"

"The soap recipe hung on a wall. The assistant from the village brought it. Her name was Koitek. Technical assistant. She took off, too. To Berlin. Besides the recipe, another notice written by von Bergen hung on the wall. It outlined the method for cleaning bones to make skeletons. But the bones weren't useful. They deteriorated. Either the temperature was too high or the fluid too strong." He still worried about these old problems.

"The soap made according to the recipe was always effective. Except once—the last batch on the table in the smokehouse.

"The soap was manufactured in the smokehouse. Doctor Spanner oversaw it personally, along with von Bergen. It was von Bergen who'd collect the corpses. Did I go with him? Yes. Twice. And once to the prison in Gdańsk.

"They brought in corpses from the mental asylum first, but still there was a shortage. So Spanner wrote to all the mayors requesting that they not bury corpses; the Institute would send for them. Corpses arrived from the camp at Stutthoff, from the death chamber at Königsberg, from Elbląg and the Pomorze region. It was only when a guillotine was erected in the Gdańsk prison that there was no longer a shortage of corpses . . .

"Most of the corpses were Poles. But once we got German soldiers, decapitated during a ceremony in the prison. And once they brought in four or five corpses with Russian surnames."

Von Bergen always trucked in the cadavers at night.

"What kind of ceremony was it?"

"The 'launching' of the guillotine in the prison. Spanner and a few others had been invited. Spanner took von Bergen and me. Why me, I don't know. I hadn't been invited. The guests arrived by car and on foot. They entered this hall. But we stayed back and waited. We'd already examined the guillotine and the gallows. Four German soldiers had been sentenced to death. Apparently a German priest blessed it.

"I saw them drag in one prisoner. His hands were chained behind his back and his feet were bare and black. And he was stripped naked down to his underpants.

"There was a purple curtain, and behind it was another room. And the public prosecutor. The older prepper spoke later with the executioner and told us about it. So they heard the prosecutor speaking, some noise and scuffling about, the stamping of feet, as if someone were running. The blade struck. The executioner reported the sentence carried out. We saw four bodies carried out in an open coffin.

"Was there a priest at the blessing? I don't know. But they said that one of the men dressed in a soldier's uniform was a priest.

"Once von Bergen and Wohlmann transported a hundred corpses from that prison.

"But later, Spanner wanted corpses with the heads intact. He didn't want those that had been shot, either, because they required too much work and the stench was unbearable. For instance, one German soldier who'd been sentenced to death had a broken and shot-up leg. He didn't have a head, either. Everything at once. At least the corpses from the insane asylum had heads.

"Spanner always hid the surplus cadavers. Later on, he had to dig into the supply of headless cadavers.

"The big, headless sailor came from the Gdańsk prison. The corpses are cut in half because they wouldn't fit whole into the cauldron. They didn't want to fit.

"One man gives maybe five kilos of fat. The fat was stowed away in the stone basins in the smokehouse. How much?"

He ponders a long while. He wants to be as precise as possible.

"One and a half hundredweights."

Immediately, however, he adds: "That was long ago. Later it was less. When they began to retreat to the Reich—maybe only one hundredweight . . .

"Soap production was carried out in secret. Spanner forbade us to tell even the students. But they peeked in, maybe after they told one another, so they probably knew . . . Once they even called in four students from the smokehouse to cook it up. But as a rule, only Spanner, the older prepper, me, and two German workers had daily access to the production. Spanner disposed of the cooked soap himself.

"Cooked soap? . . . No, it's not like that. First, it's soft, so it has to cool. Then we'd cut it . . . Spanner locked it up along with the machine. There were five of us. And the others had to specially request the key whenever they wanted to enter."

"Why was it a secret?"

He ponders over that question for a longer while, wanting to respond to the best of his ability.

"Maybe Spanner was afraid or . . ." He considers the matter carefully. "I think that if some civilian from town had found out, there might have been trouble. . . ."

Perhaps even here it seemed that a purple curtain was hanging between us and him. There was nothing we could do.

Someone finally asked, "Didn't anyone ever tell you that making soap from human fat was a crime?"

He retorted with complete frankness, "No one told me that."

This, however, gives him cause to think. He stops responding immediately to the remaining questions. In the end, he answers reluctantly.

"Of course people visited the Institute and Spanner. Professors Klotz, Schmidt, Rossmann. Once the Ministers of Health and Pedagogy, and even Gauleiter Forste, stopped by. As rector of the Medical Academy, Professor Grossman greeted them. Before they erected this house, it was only the Anatomy Institute that they visited to see how it functioned and whether anything was needed. Even after the smokehouse was built, the soap was always cleaned up after four or five days. I can't say for sure if they ever saw that soap. They might have. And during the inspection, the recipe was always hanging. So when they read it, perhaps they figured out what was going on there.

"Yes, the chief ordered me to make soap with the workers. Why me? I don't know. When Spanner locked up the soap, I thought he was doing something odd. If he was going to write about soap in his book, then he wouldn't have forbidden us to talk about it. Maybe he came up with the idea to make soap out of the remains by himself? . . . Maybe he didn't have any authorization, because then he wouldn't have to try to come up with the recipe himself . . ."

Nothing substantial comes from this speculation.

"The students? . . . They were just like us. In the beginning, they felt a bit uneasy about washing with the soap. The soap was disgusting. It didn't smell very good. Professor Spanner tried hard to get rid of the smell. He wrote away to chemical factories for oils. But you could always tell the soap was different.

"Of course I talked about it at home . . . In the beginning, one friend knew about it. I used to get the creeps thinking about washing myself with it. Mother was disgusted, too. But it cleaned well, so she used it for the laundry. I got used to it because it was good . . ."

A patient smile flickers across his thin, pale face.

"In Germany, you can say, people know how to make something—from nothing . . ."

3

At the inquest that afternoon we called the professors, Spanner's colleagues. The conversation took place in their jurisdiction, in the empty hall of a hospital building.

Both—interrogated separately—testified that they had no prior knowledge of the existence of the building housing the hidden soap factory. They inspected it for the first time that morning and the sight of it had shocked them.

Both—interrogated separately—testified that Spanner, a man of forty at most, was considered an expert in the field of pathology. Having known him only a short time and having seen him only on rare occasions, they couldn't say much about his moral character. They knew only that he belonged to the Party.

Each witness sat removed from us on his own chair, clearly dejected. Each sat, not having taken off his black coat, holding his black hat on his knee.

Both spoke prudently and cautiously. Both carefully weighed their words before speaking. Gdańsk, that May, was still full of Germans. Columns of German POWs marched along the streets as their women tossed flowers. But the authorities were Polish and Soviet troops were stationed in the garrison.

When asked, however, whether, knowing Spanner and his scientific activities, they could believe him capable of manufacturing soap from the bodies of dead prisoners and POWs, each responded differently.

The tall, thin one, with the gray hair and noble features, stated after careful consideration: "Yes, I could believe it, if I'd known that he'd received such an order. It was common knowledge that he was an obedient Party member."

The thick-set, good-natured one, with the ruddy jowls, also contemplated long and hard. Afterward, as though weighing everything in his conscience, he answered: "Of course, I might suspect it. For this reason. At that time, Germans were experiencing a severe shortage of fat. Given Germany's economic state, he could have been tempted to do it for the good of the nation."

The Hole

S o, what should I tell you first?" she ponders for a moment. "I don't
know myself."

She's gray-haired, rather lovely, round, soft—and worn out. What
she's lived through, no one would believe. Neither would she, except
that it's true.

She asks only for some compassion. People should take pity on her,
because she's endured so much, and she's a mother who's lost two
children. No, she's not certain they're dead. But there's been no news
of them for a very long time.

Her son still hasn't come back from the camps. And the friends
who have say that they've not seen him. As for her daughter . . .

That's a much more difficult matter. Tears escape from her big,
gentle, gray eyes. Tears come easily, only to disappear, without falling
on her cheeks.

She knows nothing about her husband either. He was last seen at
the camp in Pruszków. But then he was already an older man. Older,
although he was three years younger than she.

She's completely alone. And people should take some pity on her.
The elderly here, who remember her, yes, of course. But the young
just think she'd better not get in their way.

"So, what should I tell you first?" she repeats, blinking her eyes
from fatigue. "In Ravensbruck, they tortured us, of course. They tortured us with injections, they did experiments on women, cut open
wounds . . . And those were the doctors who did that, the intelligentsia. But we didn't stay there long. Just three weeks. We were transferred to another camp, to a munitions factory.

"My daughter as well. Of course. We stuck together everywhere.
They arrested us at the same time. It was only on the way back that

we lost each other. They detained her and also a couple of other girls—maybe ten in total."

She speaks in a voice hushed by quick, simple words that fall easily and sadly. The memories of her daughter are many. She was good. She was pretty. She was talented. She taught children and belonged to clubs. Her son, too. They were frightened those nights he'd return home late, long past curfew. He'd toss stones against the window; they'd let down the rope so he could climb in so as to avoid being spotted by the watchman. She'd tremble, afraid that someone would finally see this, that they would be found out.

They arrested him as well, but not with them. He was captured during the uprising. The last note he wrote to his family was dated January. He knew that his mother and sister had long since been in Germany.

"Before the camp, we spent two months in Pawiak. The things they did, the criminal acts they performed on people! Injections, taking blood for soldiers—and then hanging or shooting them. They never shot the healthy ones. Only those to whom they'd already done everything they could."

It's obvious she passed over much in silence.

"I know because the men who cooked in the kitchen, they told us. They also mentioned the rats . . . The prisoners themselves had to carry out the bodies in the morning, hands and legs bound, insides gnawed out. A few with their hearts still beating."

Again she pondered over something she couldn't say out loud. The memory drew a barely perceptible crease across her smooth forehead.

"They didn't torture me so much as beat me a lot," she said finally.

Again, subdued, quick, small words poured out.

"They beat me up badly to force me to tell them who visited, what the ones who supposedly came for dance lessons where my daughter played the piano really did. They beat me with a rubber cudgel . . . When I covered my face with my hands, they'd hit my fingers with the cudgel. Here, you can still see. They still hurt when I do any work."

She displayed her bruised hands, her delicate, smallish hands ruined by hard labor.

"I was dreadfully afraid that I'd say something when it would hurt too much and I'd almost faint. But somehow I made up my mind, somehow I hardened myself, and I didn't say anything."

She sighed with relief and added trustingly: "They studied at our home. They carried cudgels instead of carbines. My son taught them."

She started. She covered her eyes with those delicate, shapeless hands and said, "Now I'll tell you what it was like in the munitions factory. We worked at the machines for twelve hours a day.

"We slept in the camp—Bunzig, the new camp was called. From there we had a two-kilometer walk to the factory. They woke us up at three A.M. There was no light. We made our beds in the dark, drank black coffee without sugar, and wolfed down our bread. Roll call was from four to five-thirty outside. Cold, rain, snow, it didn't matter. Then the half-hour walk to the factory to be there by six. We ate lunch at the factory. Soup made from leaves or something. I can't explain. Dried turnips, or some such thing. Morning and evening, black coffee, no sugar, and one hundred grams of bread for the whole day. At first, they gave us a hundred and fifty, but later only a hundred. It was such a small piece. So we were always hungry. The hunger was unbearable.

"We mostly manufactured bullets for guns—aircraft and antiaircraft guns. It was hard work, what with the smoke and heat. Whenever one of the women couldn't fill her quota, we were all punished.

"How? There were bunkers in the camp—isolated, far apart, freezing, consisting of just a bit of earth, like a cellar. If someone didn't make her bed or clean her coffee cup properly, because there was no water and, of course, it was dark, she had to go to the bunker. Or stand for twelve hours in the frost or rain. The Gestapo would walk around, watching, laughing at us freezing to death. If we turned to each other for warmth, they'd beat us or send us to the bunker as punishment. So we were forced to stand far apart from each other in that cold. We wore summer dresses—not our own, either. They stole ours. These were camp issue, these were ordinary dresses, with sleeves down to the elbow, and our legs were bare. The backs were sewn crosswise with strips.

"Twice they shaved my head bald and I had to go outside in the frost like that. I wasn't allowed to cover my head. They beat me right away. Our shoes were wooden, fastened only with some paper at the toes so they'd stay on. Our legs were such a livid blue, as if they'd been painted.

"The winter was extremely harsh. All the weaker ones died alongside the road or working at the machines. The corpses were stacked in the bunkers. It was in those very bunkers that people would be locked up for any minor offense. No food, no blanket. All night long on that bare earth. They'd be let out only in the morning at roll call, but afterward, it was right back to the bunker without food. We were forbidden to give them any. They'd stand at attention, apart from everyone, so no one could share her bread with them. The SS women were extremely diligent in that . . ."

She hesitated, considered carefully. Again she had something to tell that was difficult.

"They did eat, though," she said quietly. "Once, one of them moved her jaw. Another had bloodied fingernails. Please, madame, that was severely punished! But at night they would eat the flesh of those corpses!"

She fell silent and remained so for a long time. She pondered, as though she wanted to add something. But she couldn't. She shook it off.

"The SS women were just delighted when we would die," she drew out in a steadier voice, as though having overcome some temptation. "When the women died standing at roll call and would keel over, the SS wouldn't believe it. They'd smirk and kick them, as if they were faking it. They'd kick them, even though they'd been dead well over a quarter-hour. We had to stand to the side. We were forbidden to budge. We were forbidden to offer any help. We couldn't do anything.

"When someone would fall ill, they'd say she was faking it. And they'd throw her in the bunker so she could die among the corpses. And the men's bunkers were even worse, completely underground. They had to stand in freezing water up to their knees."

She sat motionless, mulling over something else. Suddenly she revived.

"I'll tell you something else, madame. This is interesting. When they took us from Pawiak—this is very interesting—they gave us each a loaf of bread and drove us to Ravensbruck in cattle cars. They loaded us up by the hundreds into the wagons, packing us in tight.

"No water, no way to leave; we could only stand. We slept standing up; we were packed in so tight we couldn't even crouch down. For seven whole days.

"Along the way, we pulled over at a side track. The train stood motionless for three hours. Then we all began to howl for water. Trapped in that lead-sealed boxcar, baking in the heat, soaked in sweat, our faces black and dusty, our clothing stinking, our legs filthy with shit. So we started to howl like animals.

"Then a German officer from another train, which was transporting wounded soldiers, walked over and ordered the wagon opened. But the Ukrainians convoying us said that it was prohibited, that they were transporting criminals. Then he called over some other officers because he was curious about what was inside. They unlocked the wagon. Then they saw us.

"Madame! When he saw us, his eyes grew round, he threw up his arms like so in fright. Oh, he was afraid of *us!* He looked like a wild boar!

"After a moment, he asked if one of the women spoke German or French. Several did. He ordered them to bring water to us and that we be let out so we could clean ourselves up. He also ordered the men's cattle cars opened. It was even worse there. There were only fifteen hundred women, but apparently four thousand men. At least three to four hundred in each wagon had suffocated to death!"

She calmed down, having related the most interesting incident. She quietly finished her tale, her voice exhausted.

"Then they locked us up again, and the doors stayed sealed for the rest of the trip to Ravensbruck. Even though no one suffocated to death, a few did go mad. Did they get well later? No. They didn't. Immediately on arrival at Ravensbruck, they were shot.

"When they went mad, they'd throw themselves on us, biting and tearing at us. One of them, who'd kept silent at Pawiak, suddenly divulged the locations of buried weapons, in a forest, at a crossroads, in some village. She said whatever came into her head. We were afraid she would lose it completely. But they didn't bother listening. They just shot them. One after the other."

She grew sad.

"It's scary, but I don't remember their names. They were worthy, decent women. Maybe their families are searching for them even as we speak, just as I'm looking for my children. And I can't even remember who they were.

"You see, madame, you see! Even the German was frightened when he saw us. Why is it so incomprehensible, then, that the women couldn't withstand it?"

The Cemetery Lady

The road to the cemetery leads through the town along that wall. All the windows and balconies, once crowded with immured, watchful people, are vacant. For a long time now, one could see the same, open, second-story window and, past the crimson curtain hanging from a sagging cornice, a dried flower in its pot of crumbled clay, and the ever-open doors of a cheap credenza standing against a wall.

Months pass and no one lifts the cornice or shuts the credenza doors.

The road leads from this living town to the place of the dead. Yet, though framed by vacancy, the cemetery is not completely outside life—as we shall see and hear.

Above the fresh, young greenery of the cemetery trees, smoke curls and branches upward in black clouds. At times, it is pierced by a long, flamelike, scarlet sash flashing in the wind. And beyond, the sky reverberates with the grumble of airplanes.

Months pass and nothing changes. It goes on.

News of the dead reaches us from all sides. P. was killed in the camp; K., having been captured on the street and taken away, died at some small railway station. People disappear in every manner, under every possible pretext. It seems there is no one alive, no reason to struggle. No shortage of death here. In the cemetery chapel vaults, caskets stand in rows, as if in a queue, awaiting burial. Ordinary, private death, next to the immensity of collective death, seems rather improper. Yet to live is an even greater impropriety.

Nothing of the past world is real. Nothing has remained. People are made to survive what seems to lie beyond their capability. Fear ultimately divides them—fear that the other may cause their death.

Still, reality is endurable because it is selective. It draws near in fragmented events and tattered reports, in echoing shots, in the distant smoke drifts, in the fires which, history cryptically says, "turn into ashes." This reality, at once distant and played out against the wall, is not real—that is, until the mind struggles to gather it up, arrest, and understand it.

Once again, we walk along the cemetery avenue. A solemn, vernal reception for the dead is being held. In the name of those who died long ago and of an ordinary death.

They confide only their names, the date, sometimes their occupation and title. Rarely, and only in whispered tones, do they offer a silent prayer to God. They are always there, in the same place, uttering the same thing, answering with self-restraint, constrained by their own conventions. They want so little, neither imposing themselves nor obligating us to anything. They scarcely recall their memories; a modicum of attention suffices.

Occasionally, a close family member offers encouragement, ushers them in, and supports them. Some anonymous wife with her children, offering this memorial to her husband, utters, in a stony whisper, that he was the best. A daughter, who has herself long since passed away, vows affection to her beloved mother in the mossy letters.

One grave has no cross. On the plinth of the bronze memorial, these now unintelligible words are carved out:

GAZING FROM THIS MOST EXALTED POSITION IN
EVOLUTION
INTO THE INFINITE ABYSS OF THE FUTURE,
WE DISCERN THERE
NOT THE DESPERATE DUSKS OF ETERNAL DEATH,
BUT THE VIVIFYING FLASH
OF ETERNAL AND OMNIPOTENT LIFE.

The woman who tends the flowers on the graves approaches along the row of the dead. In her hands, she carries the emblems of her station: the broom and pitcher. She places the pitcher on a flat stone by the iron well and pumps water into it.

The cemetery next to the hedge is drowned in greenery. Graves lie like dwarfed beds of indigo and yellow pansies. Fragrant lilies bloom;

soon the lilacs will also be in bloom. In this green breeze, a yellow thrush calls, as it has called each spring at the childhood home. A field mouse trips lightly among the pansies and, clinging to their stems, nibbles away at something.

Every fifteen minutes from the airport, a slow airplane ascends the silent expanse above the cemetery and, tracing out a gentle half-circle, veers off behind the ghetto walls. Invisible bombs drop in silence. After a long while, spirals of smoke curl upward in the traces of flight and dissipate. Later, flames can be seen.

Having filled up the pitcher, the cemetery lady heads toward the flowers. It is with her that one speaks about death.

In times of danger, the cemetery is the one place of refuge—like the garden at the family home, like the most certain address.

She shook even my certainty.

"The graves are better here," she informed me. "The graves are better here because it's dry. The body doesn't rot. It just dries out. Down below, where it's wet, the plots are cheaper. Just two coffins can lie there, one on top of the other."

She had a gentle, tender disposition. Moreover, she was competent. She always dispensed advice, even compassion. She was round and pale, not much could upset her, forbearing as she was toward everything.

"And it's higher here," she continued. "When they dug up one woman, she hadn't changed a bit. The husband requested it. She was young, buried in a white dress. And the dress was still completely white. Like she'd been buried yesterday."

It wasn't clear just why he'd requested the exhumation.

She explained: "They dug her up because he accused the hospital doctors of not providing proper care. After bearing her first child, she jumped out the window and killed herself. There was no one watching over her as there should have been. So they dug her up and took her to the hospital to examine her. And later they brought her back and buried her. But she wasn't wearing the white dress anymore. Just a blue one."

They buried her, but not for long. Three months had scarcely passed when they again removed the coffin.

"Why?"

"Because the husband hanged himself and they had to bury him.

They deepened the grave, supporting the sides with a wall. And now they're resting there together."

How the affair against the doctors really ended is also unclear. Apparently, however, the outcome hadn't assuaged the husband's grief, so he sought to escape his suffering in death.

The time came when shells dropped on the cemetery. Shattered statues and medallions lay along the avenue. Opened graves displayed their dead.

Yet, even when confronted with this sight, the cemetery lady preserved her natural poise.

"Nothing will happen to them," she commented. "They can't die twice."

However, when she returned with the water this time, a change was noticeable.

"What's wrong? Are you ill?"

Her naturally round, pale face was flushed and shrunken, her forehead wrinkled as if from constant exertion, her eyes feverishly bright.

"No, no, nothing like that," she responded darkly. "It's just . . . people just can't live here anymore."

Even her voice was uncertain, quivering, and muffled.

"We all live right by the wall, you see, so we can hear what goes on there. Now we all know. They shoot people in the streets. Burn them in their homes. And at night, such shrieks and cries. No one can eat or sleep. We can't stand it. You think it's pleasant listening to all that?"

She glanced around warily as if the graves of the empty cemetery were listening.

"They're human beings after all, so you have to feel sorry for them," she explained. "But they despise us more than they do the Germans."

She seemed offended by my naive words.

"What do you mean, 'Who said that?' No one had to say anything. I know myself. And anyone who knows them will tell you the same thing . . . If the Germans lose the war, the Jews will kill us all. You don't believe me? Listen, even the Germans say so . . . and the radio, it says so too."

She knew best why she needed to believe this.

She placed the pitcher on the stone again and pumped more water.

When she finished, she lifted her head, wrinkled her forehead, and squinted her eyes in distress.

"We just can't bear it. We can't bear it . . . ," her words echoed. With trembling hands, she started to wipe away the easy tears from her face.

"What's worse is that they can't be saved." She spoke in a hushed tone, as if she feared being overheard. "They kill them on the spot if they defend themselves. And those who don't, they transport just as surely as to their death. So what can we do? They set them on fire and lock them up in their homes. The mothers wrap up their children in anything soft and throw them out the window onto the pavement below. Then they jump too. Some even jump holding the youngest child."

She edged closer.

"From one spot in our home, you could watch a father jump with a small boy. He coaxed him, but the boy was scared. He just stood there in the window and clung to the frame. And whether the father shoved him or what, you couldn't tell. But they both fell down, one after the other."

And again she let loose some tears and wiped her face with trembling hands.

"Even when we don't see it, we hear it . . . it's like something soft smacking down. Thwack, thwack . . . each time they jump—and they'd rather jump than be burned to death."

She listened intently. In the soft appeal of the cemetery birds, she could make out the muffled sound of bodies falling on the pavement. Lugging the pitcher, she headed toward the yellow and indigo pansies on the graves. From the airport, another plane approached and, in a great circular motion, reached the ghetto walls.

Reality is bearable when something prevents us from knowing it completely. It draws near in fragmented events, in tattered reports. We know of the peaceful death marches of unresisting people. Of the leaps into flame, of the leaps into the abyss. But, then, we are on this side of the wall.

The cemetery lady knew and heard, too. But, for her, the matter was interjected with so many commentaries that it had lost its reality.

By the Railway Track

Yet another person now belongs to the dead: the young woman by the railway track whose escape attempt failed.

One can make her acquaintance only through the tale of a man who had witnessed the incident but is unable to understand it. She lives on only in his memory.

Those who were being transported to extermination camps in the lead-sealed boxcars of the long trains would sometimes escape en route. Not many dared such a feat. The courage required was even greater than that needed to go hopelessly, unresisting and meek, to a certain death.

Sometimes the escape would succeed. The deafening clatter of the rushing boxcars prevented those on the outside from hearing what went on inside.

The only means of escape was by ripping up the floorboards. In the cramp of jammed-in, starved, foul-smelling, filthy people, it seemed an improbable gambit. Even to move was impossible. The beaten human mass, wriggling with the rushing rhythm of the train, reeled and rocked in the suffocating stench and gloom. Nevertheless, even those who, weak and fearful, would never dream of escaping themselves understood their obligation to help others. They'd lean back, pressing against one another, and lift their shit-covered legs in order to open a way to freedom for others.

Successfully prying open one end of the floorboard raised a glimmer of hope: A collective effort was required to tear it up. It took hours. Then there remained still the second and the third boards.

Those closest would lean over the narrow aperture, then back away fearfully. Courage was called for to crawl hand and foot through the chink into the din and crash of iron, into the gale of the smoking wind below, above the gliding bases, to reach the axle and, in this catch-hold, to crawl to the spot from which jumping would guarantee the best chance at salvation. To drop somehow, some way, in between the rails or through the wheels. Then, to recover one's senses, roll down unseen from the mound, and escape into the strange, temptingly dark forest.

People would often fall under the wheels and be killed on the spot, struck by a protruding beam, the edge of a bar, thrown forcefully against a signal pole or roadside rock. Or they'd break their arms and legs, and be delivered thus unto the greater cruelty of the enemy.

Those who dared to step into the roaring, crashing, yawning mouth were aware of what they risked. Just as those who remained behind were, even though there was no possibility of looking out through the sealed doors or high-set windows.

The woman lying by the track belonged to those who dared. She was the third to step through the opening in the floor. A few others rolled down after her. At that moment a volley of shots rang out over the travelers' heads—an explosion on the roof of the boxcar. Suddenly the shots fell silent. The travelers could now regard the dark place left by the ripped-up boards as though it were the opening to a grave. And they could ride on calmly, ever closer to their own death, which awaited them at the crossroads.

The smoke and rattle of the train had long since disappeared into the darkness.

All that remained was the world.

The man, who can neither understand nor forget, relates his story once again.

When the new day broke, the woman was sitting on the dew-soaked grass by the side of the track. She was wounded in the knee. Some had succeeded in escaping. Further from the track, another lay motionless in the forest. A few had escaped. Two had died. She was the only one left like this, neither alive nor dead.

She was alone when he found her. But slowly people started to appear in that empty space, emerging from the brick kiln and village. Workers, women, and a boy stood fearful, watching her from a distance.

Every once in a while, a small chain of people would form. They'd cast their eyes about nervously and quickly depart. Others would approach, but wouldn't linger for long. They would whisper among themselves, sigh, and walk away.

The situation was clear. Her curly, raven hair was obviously disheveled, her too-dark eyes overflowed the lowered lids. No one uttered a word to her. It was she who asked if the ones in the forest were alive. She learned they weren't.

The day was white. The space open onto everything as far as the eye could see. People had already learned of the incident. It was a time of terror. Those who offered assistance or shelter were marked for death.

She begged one young man, who was standing for a while longer, then started to walk away, only to turn back, to bring her some Veronal from the pharmacy. She offered him money. He refused.

She lay back for a while, her eyes shut. Then she sat up again, shifted her leg, clasped it with both hands, and brushed her skirt from her knee. Her hands were bloodied. Her shattered knee a death sentence. She lay quietly for a long time, shutting her too-black eyes against the world.

When she finally opened them again, she noticed new faces hovering around her. The young man still lingered. So she asked him to buy her some vodka and cigarettes. He rendered her this service.

The gathering beside the mound attracted attention. Someone new would latch on. She lay among people but didn't count on anyone for help. She lay like an animal that had been wounded during a hunt but which the hunters had forgotten to kill off. She proceeded to get drunk. She dozed. The power that cut her off from all the others by forming a ring of fear was unbeatable.

Time passed. An old village woman, gasping for breath, returned and, drawing near, stole a tin cup of milk and some bread from beneath her kerchief. She bent over, furtively placed them in the wounded woman's hand, and left immediately, only to look on from a distance to check whether she would drink the milk. It was only when she noticed two policemen approaching from the village that she disappeared, drawing her scarf across her face.

The others dispersed, too. Only the slick, small-town guy who had brought her the vodka and cigarettes continued to keep her company. But she no longer wanted anything from him.

The police came to see what was going on. They quickly sized up the situation and deliberated on to how to handle it. She begged them to shoot her. In a low voice, she tried to negotiate with them, provided they keep the whole thing quiet. They were undecided.

They, too, left, conferred, stopped, and walked on further. What they would finally decide was not certain. In the end, however, they did not care to carry out her request. She noticed that the kind young man, who had lit her cigarettes with a lighter that didn't want to light, followed after. She had told him that one of the two dead in the forest was her husband. That piece of news seemed to have caused him some unpleasantness.

She tried to swallow the milk but, preoccupied, set the cup down on the grass. A heavy, windy, spring day rolled over. It was cool. Beyond the empty field stood a couple of huts; at the other end, a few short, scrawny pines swept the sky with their branches. The forest, their destination, sprang up further from the railway. This emptiness was the whole of the world she saw.

The young man returned. She swallowed some more vodka and he lit her cigarette. A light dusk brushed across the sky from the east. To the west, skeins and smudges of clouds branched up sharply.

More people, on their way home from work, turned up and were told what had happened. They spoke as though she couldn't hear them, as though she were no longer there.

"The dead one there's her husband," a woman's voice spoke up.

"They tried to escape from the train into the forest. But they shot at them with a rifle. They killed her husband, and she was left alone. Shot in the knee. She couldn't get any further . . ."

"From the forest she could easily have been taken somewhere. But here, with everyone watching, there's no way."

The old lady who had returned for her tin cup said those words. Silently she watched as the milk soaked into the grass.

So no one would intercede by removing her before nightfall, or by calling a doctor, or by taking her to the station so she could get to a hospital. Nothing of the kind would happen. She could only die, one way or another.

When she opened her eyes at dusk, there was no one around except for the two policemen who had come back and the one who would no longer go away. Again she pleaded with them to kill her, but without any expectation that they would do so. She covered her eyes with her hands so as not to see anymore.

The policemen still hesitated about what to do. One tried to talk the other into doing it. The latter retorted, "You do it yourself."

Then she heard the young man's voice saying, "Well then give it to me."

Again they debated, quarreled. From beneath her lowered eyelids she watched the policeman take out his revolver and hand it to the stranger.

A small group of people standing further back watched as he bent over her. They heard the shot and turned away in disgust.

"They could at least have called in someone. Not do it like that. Like she was a dog."

When it grew dark, two people emerged from the forest to get her. They located the spot with a bit of difficulty. They assumed she was sleeping. But when one of them took her by the shoulder, he understood at once that he was dealing with a corpse.

She lay there all that night and into the morning, until just before noon, when a bailiff arrived and ordered her buried together with the other two who had died by the railway tracks.

"Why he shot her isn't clear," the narrator said. "I couldn't understand it. Maybe he felt sorry for her. . . ."

Dwojra Zielona

A smallish woman with a black eye patch stood next to the counter. Her equally slight, rather odd-looking companion with a black mustache was requesting glasses for her.

"For two years this woman did not wear glasses," he said in a deliberate yet friendly tone.

"Why?"

"Because she was in a camp."

As for the glass eye, it turned out not to be suitable. It was too big and did not fit. They were to come back the day after tomorrow for the glasses.

"I'd like to talk with you. We could step into the pastry shop next door."

She was surprised. She couldn't go to the pastry shop. She was busy. She had to return to the apartment, because it was locked and she had the key with her. To the apartment where two days before she had found work.

We strolled together along the broad street of the Prague district, passed through the dark gate, and entered the courtyard of a huge, dilapidated building with dirty, blackened walls of crumbling plaster. The gloomy entry was recessed deep in the corner, past the doors of peeling brown paint.

"It's on the third floor."

The wooden steps led upward in the dark with an unbroken continuity. One had to grope for the handrail, feeling carefully with one's feet for any gaps in the boards so as not to stumble. Only the first floor interrupted the constant course. The even platform wound back to the spot where the stairs began again, and again, in one long breath, they reached up to the second floor.

At the entrance to the third floor, we stopped for a moment by the window to peer into the great, ragged gloom and filth of the courtyard.

"What do you do?"

"I clean and take care of the apartment. A Jewish infirmary will be here."

"So you found your people? You have someone to take care of you? Friends?"

"I'm alone." She responds quickly. "I'm alone," she reiterates.

"But that man bought you glasses. And an eye."

She acquiesced with some difficulty.

"Of course, they buy me this eye. And they want even to fix my teeth," she hesitated and acknowledged despondently. "But this is not family."

We reached the last apartment and, again, wound our way back along the even gangway, bordered by a wooden railing. In the spot where there were windows on a lower level, here faded, crooked French doors opened out onto a wooden balcony attached to the wall and cracking in the emptiness.

We stopped before the third, shuttered door.

"Here it is," she says.

She took out her key and thrust it into a huge padlock. The door opened onto a spacious, empty apartment. The first room, its floor washed, lay empty and gloomy. In the second room, which was clean, a low couch had been pushed against the wall. In the third stood a table and two chairs.

"Here, we can talk here. Sit down, please."

We sat at the table across from one another.

"They are good people. But this is not family," she repeated. "I have no one. My husband, he was killed in 1943 at Małaszewicze station, eight kilometers from Brest-Litovsk. In the camp. A thousand were killed then because they were killing every tenth person. They killed every few days. No, I didn't see it myself, but I heard about it. Because I wasn't there. I was in Międzyrzecz. I know only that my husband was still alive in 1942. A German airman took a letter to him and to that letter came an answer that my husband sends regards. Later I learned he was dead."

She got up to let in some workers who had come to fix the kitchen sink.

"I'm thirty-five years old. I know I don't look it. I don't have teeth. I'm missing an eye . . ."

She had married at the age of twenty-three. They lived in Warsaw on Stawka Street. She used to work in a factory that manufactured woolen gloves. He had been a shoemaker. He worked in a factory at first as well, but later he had his own cobbler's shop at home. Of course, it had been a difficult period for them. They had no children.

"My husband was called Rayszer, but I'm called Zielona. I didn't have documents, so they gave me my father's surname."

After a moment of consideration, she added, "And Dwojra is my first name."

In 1939, the bombs destroyed their home on Stawka. They lost everything—all their belongings, all their clothing. Then they moved to Janów Podlaski.

She sighed.

"There we already were wearing the yellow triangle, with its six points—the Palestine mark. Only later did we wear the armbands. Both of us."

In October 1942, her husband was no longer there because he was working in the camp at Małaszewicze. Then the entire town of Janów Podlaski was resettled to Międzyrzecz. It became a Judenstadt. All the Jews from the Lublin province were moved there. Every two weeks, they would transport people to Treblinka by train. Those who remained behind were locked up in the ghetto. Others perished. Not she.

"When there was an action, I hid. I sat on the roof."

She shielded her face with her extended fingers. With her one eye, she peers through the chinks between her fingers.

"Does that mean that you hid your face with your hands?"

She smiled. "Ach, no. I'm showing you only that I always hid like that."

She sat on the roof and thought, "Now I'm alive, but I don't know what will be in an hour." Others died. Not she.

"I once hid like that for four whole weeks when there was an action. Without eating."

This too, like the outstretched fingers on the face, was to be understood metaphorically.

"Well, I did take a couple of onions, and I had some kasha, so I did eat. No, it wasn't cooked. How? There wasn't any water. I had some ground chicory coffee also—I ate it raw, yes, of course. Nothing bothered me. I thought, I'm going to die. I was so weak. I was all alone in the world.

"Once I heard some movement on the street. It was December 1942. I heard movement so I knew they weren't guarding the square anymore. So I went out. After the action, you could walk between the wires again. Of course, the Jewish administration still ran the ghetto. They handed out a bit of bread.

"But it wasn't important, this life of ours . . .

"I sold the few shirts I still owned to buy some bread for the next day, the day after.

"I lost my eye on the first of January 1943. The Germans had this game. They celebrated New Year's by shooting sixty-five people. From my house, I was the only one left that still lives. At six A.M., they fired on the streets, in the snow. They broke into apartments. I tried to escape. I jumped out the window. I thought I had killed myself. And I got a shot in the eye.

"When they shot me, I thought, 'Maybe I'm still alive . . .'"

She lowered her voice and added confidentially, "I'll tell you: I wanted to live. I don't know why. Because I didn't have a husband or family, no one, and I wanted to live. I was missing an eye, I was hungry and cold, and I wanted to live. Why? I'll tell you why: to tell everything just like I'm telling you now. To let the world know what they did.

"I thought, 'I'm the only one who's going to survive.' I thought, 'There won't be a single Jew left on the face of this earth.'

"They took me to the hospital. I didn't feel a thing in my eye. It hurt more here, in the back and legs. They were broken. I said, 'Give me a knife.' Because I wanted to put an end to myself. I couldn't live anymore. My eye was gone. Everything was gone. The eye fell out in one piece. I was wounded in the ear, too. They were going to x-ray it. But it healed by itself.

"When they transported the last of the Jews, I stopped hiding. I followed the others to Majdanek myself.

"I thought, 'I don't have a penny. I have nothing to eat. My eye is gone. No Jews left.' So what was I going to do by myself all alone on that roof? I didn't even have that piece of bread anymore. If I was going to die, then I preferred to die with others, not alone.

"So I went to Majdanek. They didn't give much bread there. And only a bit of soup at noon.

"Did we help each another? I don't know. A bit, yes. Not a lot. Ach, you know, everyone has his own troubles. What can you do? Every two weeks there was a selection. What could you do?

"Did they beat me? Of course. Once in Majdanek, an SS woman, Brigette, she beat me. How? She had a cudgel. I got it on the head. And for what?"

She smiles at the concern.

"Because she wanted to. No other reason.

"We all got it then. Because one Kapo, a *führabtarina,* said that one of us was doing *Geschäft.* Meaning she was buying something. And because of that one, we all got punished. But was that woman really doing *Geschäft?* Who knows?

"Escape was impossible. One girl tried. They caught her and hanged her. A pole and hook stood there . . . We were ten thousand in the square, and we all had to watch.

"She was quiet, very quiet. The SS man asked what she wanted before she died. She said, 'Nothing, nothing, just do it quickly, whatever you do.' She was twenty years old, delicate.

"There were two brothers, too. Later they hanged themselves."

She stood up in order to let out the workers who had finished their job. But she returned immediately and sat back down in her chair.

"Once an SS man from Skarżysko-Kamienna showed up. Chief Imfling. He said, 'Whoever wants to work will go to work.' I knew how to work, so I went. To a munitions factory.

"I didn't get even one beating there. But sometimes they had selections there. If someone went to the hospital just once, he was killed. Whoever had leave from work, even for just two days—he was killed.

"I had only one eye and I developed a sty on it, like an ulcer. So I was blind. But I worked. Not one day did I did take off. Twelve hours a day we worked—one week the day shift, one week the night shift. You see, I didn't take any time off. I didn't go to the doctor even once. I was scared. Because that meant death. I thought, 'Maybe I'll survive and so, and maybe . . .'"

She smiled shyly, ashamed.

"You see, again I wanted to live."

She remembered something else.

"Now I'll tell you what happened to my teeth.

"When I arrived at Skarżysko-Kamienna, they gave only a little soup. So I was starving.

"You could buy food from the workers who came from town. Sometimes they gave away food for nothing, but it was quicker to buy it. But I didn't have any money. So I pulled out my own gold teeth.

"Did I pull them out with a string? No. I just jiggled them for a few days until they could be pulled out easily. They came out by themselves. For each tooth, I got eighty or eighty-five złotys. So I could buy myself enough bread.

"I worked like that at Skarżysko for thirteen months. When the Russians neared Skarżysko, the Germans evacuated us and the entire factory to Częstochowa. We did the same type of work there.

"On January seventeenth, the Soviets arrived. The SS men had escaped on the sixteenth. At one time there were fifteen thousand Jews in Częstochowa. Only five thousand were left. They evacuated the rest to Germany by train. Nothing could be done. There were some registration lists. The foreman wrote the names down and they took people on the list.

"The foremen kept guard over us. If the Soviets had come even a couple of hours later, it would have been too late. We were already lined up in the streets. But the Soviets arrived and the foremen escaped.

"Were we happy they came? Yes, we were very happy. Because we weren't behind barbed-wire fences anymore. Because we were free. We welcomed them, but we didn't yell or anything."

She sighed, "We didn't have the strength . . ."

The Visa

I don't have an aversion to Jews. Just like I don't have an aversion to ants or mice."

She waits for a moment to gauge my reaction.

She sits with some difficulty. She's large and rather stout. She hasn't yet parted with her camp gray-and-navy-striped gabardine. Her hair is still shorn in the masculine crewcut. And she wears the same gray-and-navy-striped cap.

She's come to the hotel room for a chat. She's seated on a soft, comfortable chair. She doesn't ask for anything. She doesn't need anything. Especially money. As for the money she's been holding in trust, she wants to dispose of it as quickly as possible to whomever needs it most. As a last resort, she would give it up for safekeeping. She regards it with such disgust.

She leans two long, wooden crutches up against the arm of the chair.

"Why do I bring up mice?" she asks, although I never asked her about it. She smiles.

She has a beautiful smile that reveals lots of young, white teeth. Her brown eyes sparkle; her cheeks are flushed and ruddy.

She's young, but disfigured by the brush cut, cook's cap, and oversized glasses.

"Because once I was peeling potatoes in the barracks kitchen with a Maryvite. And in those potatoes we discovered a nest of mice. The nest was inside a potato. The whole inside was gnawed out, and they lay inside the skin. There were three young ones, completely naked, a dirty pink color. That Maryvite wanted to let the cat at them. But I wouldn't let her . . ."

She hesitates for a moment.

35

"Because a thought came to mind: how is this cat going to eat these mice?"

She adds grudgingly, "I was curious, just like the Gestapo, about how it would to look . . ."

She pondered over this particular incident longer. She appeared to look inside herself. She sighed.

"So I hid them again in the skin and buried them deep in the hay. Maybe the mother will find them and rescue them somehow."

So she really doesn't have an aversion to Jews, even though she herself is a Christian. She converted to Catholicism at the beginning of the war when the many injustices and cruelties she witnessed caused her so much suffering. Thinking about Christ helped her to bear it all more easily.

She had a Polish surname and Polish papers. She was in the camp as a Pole, not as a Jew. She doesn't know her parents; she never saw them. She knows only the grandmother who raised her. But that isn't important. Besides, her grandmother isn't alive anymore.

These circumstances also merit some consideration.

"I don't despise anyone at all. But that isn't important."

What is important is the next item.

"Do you know what it means to go on the visa?"*

"No, I don't."

"In the camp, first thing in the morning, the SS women would yell out, 'On the *wiese!* On the *wiese!*' . . . And the Yugoslavs would say, *'Iti na luku . . .'*

"It was October. The days were very cold and wet. All the women from one barrack went on the visa. And they stayed there until evening. Because the barrack had to be cleaned.

"As for the visa, it's a meadow right by the forest, under the trees. They stood there in the cold all day without eating and without any work. The barrack had to be clean, and the tidying up and disinfection lasted several days. So in the meantime, they just stood there. I don't know how many there were. A lot. The Germans probably hated them so much because there were so many of them. . . . French,

---

Wiese means "meadow" in German, which the Yugoslav women clearly understand, but the Poles and other Slavs enjoy the dark joke of going on a "visa."—TRANS.

Dutch, Belgians, lots of Greeks. The Greeks were in the worst shape. The Poles and Russians were stronger.

"They had to squeeze together, one right up against the other, even though there was enough room. Dirty, ulcerated, cadaverous. Along with the sick and dying. They didn't bother treating them anymore . . ."

She speaks always of them, never of herself. So it isn't clear whether she was in there with them, or whether she looked on from the outside.

"Because they'd been in the camp for seven months, and we'd barely just arrived on a fresh transport. Still, we joined them on the visa on the second day. They looked ghastly, and the worst of it was there were so many of them. I knew we were going to end up the same way."

She doesn't talk about what she herself suffered. She speaks only of others.

"I wasn't afraid. I knew I was going to die, so I wasn't afraid."

About herself she says that she'd always pray when they beat her. She prayed in order not to feel hatred. For no other reason.

She doesn't say much about her disability either. Her leg hadn't healed properly so she has to undergo another operation in order to break the bone and reset it. Of course, she'll go to the hospital, but not right away. First she must take care of a few matters. She wants to go to Gdańsk to see the sea. And also to visit a friend from the camp who now lives in Poznań. She's just received a letter from her and knows that she can be of some use to the woman.

Under what circumstances she broke her leg and whether she truly did not feel any hatred then are unknown. At any rate, she will go to the hospital, only later on.

"They were chased on the visa every day for a whole week. They'd press together tightly in order to warm themselves. They'd all try to press to the inside for warmth. No one wanted to be left on the outside. They'd hunch over and hug each other as best they could. They'd always move together in a single mass . . ."

Some were covered from head to toe in ulcers because they pressed together. More and more of them died.

They were chased out all week. Until the selection.

"One day, it was cold, too, but the sun came out in the afternoon. Then they shifted toward where the trees didn't hide the sun. They shifted, not like people, but like animals. Or like in one, single mass . . .

"That day the Greeks sang a national hymn. Not in Greek. They sang a Jewish hymn in Hebrew . . . In the sunshine they sang, beautiful, loud, and strong, as though they were healthy. It wasn't physical strength, because, of course, they were the weakest. It was the strength of yearning and desire.

"On the second day, there was a selection. I came on the visa and the visa was empty."

The Man Is Strong

The palace, which no longer exists, had stood on the edge of a hill overlooking the spring landscape, divided evenly into flat green fields all the way to the horizon.

The palace was shattered, as Michael P. says, uprooted by the wind at the very moment when four crematoria were being burned down in the Żuchowski forest nearby.

It had served as an ornament, a splendid architectonic gate—a passage from life to death. It had played the role of a metaphor in a ritual long upheld with unaltered daily ceremony. People would arrive, worn out by the journey, still wearing their own traveling clothes. They would be driven through the first, then the second gate into the inner courtyard. The back doors of the truck would fall open; the travelers, helping one another, would swarm down the steps. They were still able to believe—as the sign over the entrance read—that they were entering the "Bathhouse." A moment later, they would emerge at the opposite end of the blockhouse clad only in their underwear, a few still with soap and towel in hand. Steered on by rifle butts, they would scurry up a gangplank into the mouth of the huge gas truck waiting at the rear of the palace.

The doors would slam shut. They were hermetically sealed.

It was then that those granted another fate, standing huddled in the palace cellar, would hear the terror-filled screams, the pleas, the fists beating against the truck's walls. Several minutes later, the screams would die down. The truck would lurch off. At the appropriate time, another would roll in to take its place.

The palace no longer exists. Nor do the people. At the edge of the rise grows a flat quadrangle of changing plant life, stem and leaf barely restrained by the ruins of the earthy walls. At the bottom of the precipice much of the visible world remains: the distant green fields, the May trees in the meadows, the sky-blue streaks of forest vanishing into the horizon.

A group of people gathered one sunny day on the site of the former gardens. Each was a witness to what had gone on here. A three-meter-high wooden fence had been erected around the palace. Though little was visible, one could hear when something was dragged out, when chains clattered. They would chase half-naked Jews into the bitter cold. In front of the palace, huge trucks would howl constantly as they churned toward the Żuchowski forest. Human screams were also audible.

"I lived in Ugaj. I worked for the Germans," says Michael P., a big, young Jew with an athletic build and a small head. His voice is hushed, solemn, as though he were reciting from a holy text.

"I brought my father and mother to the truck. Later, my sister and her five children, and my brother, his wife, and three children. I volunteered to ride with my parents, but they wouldn't permit me."

They had their reasons.

"My job was to tear down old barns. I had permission from the Jewish Committee at Ugaj. So I wasn't in the conspiracy when they were transporting Jews from Koła.

"A few were scared. Then Suida, a gendarme in the Polish Volks-deutsche, reassured them: 'There's nothing to be scared of. They'll take you first to Barłoga Station and then on to work.' So they stopped being afraid. A few even volunteered to go."

They transported the Jews from Koła over five days, and finished up with the sick ones. With these, the drivers were ordered to proceed slowly and carefully.

"At the beginning of January 1942, they took me and forty other Jews to the gendarmerie post in Ugaj. On the second day, a truck holding fifteen Jews drove up from Izbica. They loaded us up with the others and transported us to Chełmno. Everyone in that truck was strong, fit for heavy labor."

He gestures toward the ruins visible through the leaves.

"The palace still stood there. I was curious to see what it was like. But they forbade us to look. So, when the truck drove into the second courtyard, I looked under the canvas and caught sight of worn human rags spread out over the ground. I realized then what was going on.

"They steered us into the cellar with rifle butts. The words 'He who enters shall die' were scrawled on the wall in Yiddish.

"On the second day, they ordered me upstairs to help dispose of clothing. Men's and women's stuff, overcoats, shoes were scattered around a gallery. We transferred them to another room. And there lay already that . . . We stacked the shoes separately. Two fired ovens stood in the first room where the Jews would undress. It was warm. So they'd strip willingly.

"Even though the cellar windows had been boarded up, with a boost you could make out something through the crack.

"The Germans herded people, stripped down to their underwear, through the passage. They'd protest against having to go out naked into the cold. They realized what was waiting for them and would start to hang back. Then the Germans would shove them into the truck.

"At night, the ones who returned to the cellars from work detail reported that they were burying people in the forest—people who had been suffocated to death. It was then that I signed up to work in the forest. I thought it would be easier to escape.

"Thirty of us were driven to the Żuchowski forest. We were handed shovels and picks. At eight A.M., the first truckload from Chełmno pulled up. Those working in the trenches weren't permitted to look. But I did. When they unlocked the doors, the Germans jumped out. Dark smoke streamed out. From where we stood, you couldn't smell anything.

"Then, three Jews would climb into the truck and pitch out the corpses that were stacked about halfway up inside. A few were holding each other. Any that were still breathing would be shot in the back of the head. After dumping the corpses, the truck would head back to Chełmno.

"Afterward, two Jews would hand the corpses over to two Ukrainians in civilian clothes who'd pry out any gold teeth, yank money pouches from necks, watches from wrists, wedding rings from fingers. It was revolting, this postmortem exam.

"There were always three of them. But one day, a Ukrainian was shoved into the gas truck with the Jews. He screamed, like the others, confusing the Germans. So the one who was to inspect the Jews joined them in death.

"When the truck drove into the forest, the Ukrainian's comrades tried to revive him by performing artificial respiration. But it was no use.

"The Germans had no desire to inspect the corpses themselves, but they always kept a close watch over the Ukrainians who did. And whatever the Ukrainians would find, the Germans would store in a separate case."

They didn't order the underwear removed.

"After the inspection, we'd arrange them compactly in the trench by alternating them head to foot—face down. The trench was wider up top where approximately thirty corpses would fit. A thousand could fit in just three or four meters of ditch.

"A transport of the suffocated would arrive thirteen times a day at the forest. Each load carried up to ninety. The Jews would wipe up the floor, and any gold they came across would be stowed away in the case. Soap and towels were sent back to Chełmno.

"From the start, I urged others to escape. But everyone was depressed. Our work lasted all day while it was still light. They'd beat us to make us work faster. If someone lagged behind, they'd order him to lie face down on the corpses and shoot him in the back of the head.

"We were always guarded by the same gendarmes. They were sober, didn't talk much. Sometimes, one of them would toss a pack of cigarettes into the trench.

"Once, three German strangers showed up in the Żuchowski forest. They conferred with the SS officers, surveyed the corpses, smirked, and left.

"I worked ten days. The forest wasn't fenced off yet. Nor were there any ovens to burn corpses. Next to me, they suffocated Jews from Ugaj, Izbica; Friday, they transported in Gypsies from Łódź; Saturday, Jews from the Łódź ghetto. When these arrived, the Germans selected the twenty weakest from among us for the gas. In their place, they set to work the fresh, strong Jews from Łódź.

"The Łódź Jews were locked up in the other cellar. The first day, they asked through the wall if this was a good camp, if they give lots of bread here. When they learned the truth, they became frightened and confessed, 'We volunteered for work.'"

He falls silent. His large, bony body sags from the emotional exhaustion. After serious consideration, he breaks his silence.

"One day—Tuesday it was—the third truck arrived from Chełmno. They pitched out the bodies of my wife and children—the boy was seven, the girl, four. I lay down on my wife's body and pleaded with them to shoot me.

"They didn't oblige. One German said, 'The man is strong. He can still work hard.' And he beat me with a cudgel until I got up.

"That evening, two Jews hung themselves in the cellars. I wanted to hang myself, too, but a devout man talked me out of it.

"It was then that I planned to escape with another man during the truck ride. This time, however, he rode in the other truck. So I decided to escape by myself.

"When we reached the forest, I approached the escort for a cigarette. He obliged. I stepped back, and the others crowded him for cigarettes. I cut the canvas with a knife and jumped out. They shot at me, but missed. In the forest, a Ukrainian on a bike shot at me, but missed, too. I got away.

"I stowed away in a village barn, digging myself deep into the hay. In the morning, I overheard some peasants talking outside. They said the Germans were in the village, hunting an escaped Jew. After two days without food, I stole out of the barn. On the road, I approached a peasant whose name I don't know. He gave me some food, a cap, shaved me so I'd look human. Then, I made my way to Grabów, where I ran into the Jew with whom I'd planned to escape. He had run away the same day from the second truck."

Before departing, we were in the Żuchowski forest where the immense collective graves were being excavated—where Michael P. had once worked, and where he had recognized the bodies of his wife and children.

In the wide clearing, bounded by short, thickly overgrown pines, strips of low grasses were growing sickly. The place was bare of green heather and ferns. In one spot, a hole had been dug, and in the crumbly soil one could make out a piece of human foot. Deeper in the forest lay the site of the burned crematoria.

Two women from the region had been walking behind us in the forest. On making our acquaintance, they asked if the Commission couldn't expedite the exhumation. They were the mother and wife of a man who had been shot here when the camp had been set up. They knew where his grave was located.

Someone pointed to a tattered matchbox with Greek print. Another some rain-washed papers from a foreign pharmaceutical firm. Still another unearthed a tiny human knuckle on the site of the crematorium.

The Adults and Children of Auschwitz

As we attempt to comprehend the enormous scale of the expedited deaths and war actions that took place on Polish soil, the most powerful emotion that we experience, apart from a sense of menace, is perplexity.

Immeasurable human masses were suffocated and burned in the most scrupulously thought-out, rationalized, efficient, and perfectly organized manner possible. Of course, more self-initiated, amateurish, and personal methods were hardly discouraged either.

Not tens of thousands, not hundreds of thousands, but millions of human beings underwent manufacture into raw materials and goods in the Polish death camps. In addition to well-known spots—like Majdanek, Auschwitz, Birkenau, and Treblinka—we uncover new ones, less famous, one after the other.

Sequestered in forests, among green hills, sometimes a fair distance from the railway tracks, these spots permitted simpler and more economical systems to be set up.

So in Tuszynek and the Wiączyna suburb of Łódź, entire beds of the slaughtered have been exhumed.

One in an old palace in Chełmno, situated on a hill with a spectacular view of undulating fields of grass and grain, a second in a half-decimated silo, and yet a third in the vicinity of an extensive, dense patch of young pines, are enough to bring the number of victims to the millions.

One small, redbrick building next to the Anatomy Institute in Wrzeszcz near Gdańsk suffices for liquefying human fat into soap and flogging the skin of the murdered into parchment.

The Germans promised Jews arrested in Italy, Holland, Norway, and Czechoslovakia prime working conditions in Polish camps. Scientists were assured positions in research institutes. A certain group of Jews was even supposed to be presented with the key to the wealthy Polish industrial city of Łódź. All were advised to pack only their most precious belongings.

When the transport of prisoners reached its destination, the people would disembark on one side of the track, while their suitcases were pitched in a great heap on the opposite side.

Then they'd be ordered to strip and carefully fold their clothes before entering the bathhouse. When they'd leave this blockhouse, they would not find their own clothing. Some were steered almost naked into the gas ovens or into the hermetically sealed trucks, where they were gassed on the trip to the crematorium. Others, clad in rags, were led to work details.

As in other camps, so in Auschwitz, heaps of woolen clothing, shoes, precious articles, personal items were amassed. Trains laden with goods left for the Reich. Diamonds pried from their settings were secreted away in leather bags. Whole boxes of eyeglasses, watches, compacts, toothbrushes departed in boxcars. Everything had a value.

The utilization of burned bones for manure, of fat for soap, of skin for leather goods, of hair for mattresses—these were only the by-products of the huge state-run industry that hauled in massive revenues over the course of years.

This constant dividend flowed from human suffering and human fear, from human degradation and crime, and it became the essential economic rationale for the spectacle of the camps. The ideological postulate of exterminating races and nations served this goal, became its justification.

We learn new details from prisoners returning to Poland from the German camps of Dachau and Oranienburg, and this information augments our knowledge of the facts. It appears that in the Reich legions of specialists busied themselves with unstitching clothing and shoes transported there from the Polish camps. They discovered a huge amount of gold sewn into the seams of clothing, secreted away in the soles and heels of shoes. It comes as no surprise then that, after Himmler's death, hundreds of thousands of pounds sterling in the drafts of six nations were discovered stashed in his office under the Berchtesgaden.

Studying the unique phenomenon of Auschwitz through material made available by both eyewitness testimonials and the examination of the camps, we are struck by the fact that the system and camps were established in order to carry out a twofold task: political and economic—that is, ideal and practical.

The political task was to evacuate certain lands in order to take possession of them, including their natural resources and cultural wealth. The economic task was to ensure that this move neither proved detrimental nor incurred any costs. On the contrary, it was to ensure that it became a source of revenues: first, in terms of prisoner labor in the war-industry factories; second, in terms of the fortunes pilfered from the dead.

Such a meticulously planned and executed spectacle was the work of people. They were its executors and its victims. People dealt this fate to people.

What kind of people were they?

A queue of ex-camp prisoners filed before the Commission for the Investigation of Nazi War Crimes. Among them were scientists, politicians, doctors, professors—the pride of their respective nations.

Each was the sole survivor in his family. Each had learned of the death of his parents, wife, or children. Each had been saved without having really counted on it.

Doctor Mansfeld, a professor from the university in Budapest, declared, "I could only survive when I resigned myself to the fact that I would not be saved. If I had surrendered myself to the illusion of salvation, I would not have achieved the inner peace that allowed me to keep going."

The ethical task set for these people was to help others even while they themselves continually came up against death, even while they, too, were subjected to a wide spectrum of tortures. As doctors, they were useful to the Germans. As doctors, they possessed the means to save the victims.

So Doctor Grabczyński of Kraków transformed Holding Block No. 22 from a place of murder and terror where the sick were finished off into a real hospital. He not only ministered to their wounds, he not only procured medicines and bandages for them, but he also practiced fraud in order to prevent the gravely ill from being gassed. He saved their lives by assuring the Germans that they would be well within five days.

But even those who, of their own free will, executed the precise plan for slaughter and plunder, were people. And those "amateurs" who pushed the limits of the orders, who murdered beyond what was prescribed, were people too.

Thanks to the richly descriptive testimonials of Ambassador Mayer, who spent twelve years in the German camps, we have a picture of the Auschwitz executioners.

The worst criminal in the camp was August Glass, a thick-set, athletic man who stalked the barracks for victims on a daily basis. He would beat his prey in the kidneys so as to leave no trace, and so that death would follow within three days.

Another would place his heel on a man's throat and crush the larynx.

Yet another would plunge the prisoner's head into a vat of water until the unfortunate soul drowned.

One of the most bloodthirsty of the barrack wardens, a professional thief, was particularly exacting at roll call. As punishment for dirty clothes or boots, he would strike the individual on the head with a lead-tipped rubber cudgel with an aim that killed on the spot. His daily quota was fifteen.

Still another, six feet tall with a long nose and face, narrow eyes, a twitching Adam's apple, and apelike arms, would suffocate a few prisoners a day before breakfast, singling them out during the morning walk.

Without a doubt, these were people who could do this but didn't have to. In due time, however, everything was done in order to extract and mobilize the power that slumbered in their subconscious and that, left alone, would never have been awakened.

An unusual, painstaking selection and brilliantly conceived and executed system of education allowed those in the human drama to play out the roles destined for them.

Thanks to the testimonials of Ambassador Mayer, we know that, in the early stages, Hitler's party increased in number by recruiting its followers from among the social scum: criminals, murderers, thieves, pimps. Nazi breeding ignited their instincts. A special German law forbidding anyone from reproaching Party members for their pasts attests to this. Many who broke the law ended up rotting away in prison.

According to the testimony of a psychiatry professor from Prague,

Doctor Fischer, the Hitler Youth were schooled in sadism during special two-year courses.

Professor Fischer, an expert in justice, stated that sadism does not decrease criminal liability. These people are all conscious of their acts and must bear complete responsibility for them.

The children of Auschwitz knew that they were to die. The smallest, not yet fit to work, were selected for the gas. The selections were carried out in the following manner. The children would file under a bar hanging at a height of 1.2 meters. Fully aware of the significance of the moment, the smallest, as they approached the bar, would straighten up, step up to it on tiptoes in order to brush their heads against it and so save their lives.

Approximately six hundred children destined for the gas were held in cells until the requisite number for gassing was attained. They, too, knew what was happening. They'd scatter around the camp and hide out, but the SS men would beat them back to the barrack. Their cries for help could be heard from afar: "We don't want to go to the gas! We want to live!"

A knock came in the middle of the night at the window of one doctor. When he opened it, two boys clambered in. They were completely naked and numb from the cold. One was twelve, the other fourteen. They took the opportunity to escape from the truck at the moment it was approaching the gas chamber. The doctor hid them, fed them, procured clothing for them. Confiding in a crematorium worker, he arranged it so that the man would record clothing from two corpses more than he received. Under threat of death, he hid these boys until the time came when they could again show themselves in the camp without raising suspicion.

Doctor Epstein, a professor from Prague, was crossing the street between the barracks in Auschwitz on a pleasant summer day when he noticed two young children sitting in the sand and poking at something with a stick. He stopped and asked, "What are you doing?"

He received in reply: "We're playing at burning Jews."

❖

Jewish Lives